TORORO

BIG

DAY

Torro's Big Day is a work of fiction and has been created in association with and with permission from the Loutre Otter Café in Kyoto Japan.

Tororo, Otsuyu, Odashi, Wasabi, and Namida are based on otters appearing at the café and used as characters in this book with the express permission of the Loutre Otter Café owners.

Loutre Otter Café: Japan, 〒604-8061 Kyoto, Nakagyo Ward, Shikibucho, 259-1 舟木ビル２階

https://www.loutre-kyoto.com/

https://www.youtube.com/c/LOUTRE

Thaddeus Tuffentsamer loves to interact with his readers. You can contact him at Thaddeustuffentsamer@gmail.com

TORORO'S BIG DAY

I ALSO HAVE AN AUNTIE
NAMED ODASHI.
SHE MAKES FUNNY
FACES BUT SHE'S
REALLY SWEET!

AND MY SISTERS...

AND MY GRANDMA.
SHE'S A HUMAN, BUT WE
DON'T TELL HER THAT.

AT FIRST, I COULDN'T DO MUCH FOR MYSELF. MOM HAD TO DO EVERYTHING FOR ME.

FINALLY, MY EYES OPENED
AND MY HAIR STARTED TO
GET DARKER, JUST LIKE
MY MOM AND AUNTIES.
AND NOW I AM READY
FOR MY BIG DAY!

TO GET ME USED TO THE WATER, GRANDMA PUT ME IN THE LITTLE POOL WHERE I COULD PLAY ALL BY MYSELF.

THEN GRANDMA MADE
ME SOME CHICKEN.
I LIKE IT A LOT!

I GET TO PLAY WITH
LOTS OF TOYS.
LIKE MY SPECIAL
TUNNEL TOY.

AND NOW I SWIM WITH MY
MOM OTSUYU AND MY
AUNTIE ODASHI.
NO MORE LITTLE POOL
FOR ME!

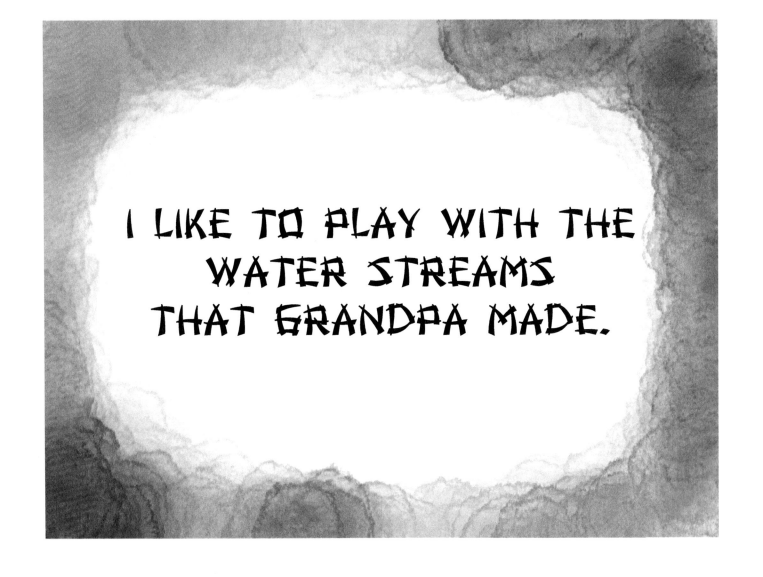

AND AFTER WE COME OUT OF THE POOL, WE PLAY IN THE TUNNEL. I HAVE THE BEST FAMILY IN THE WORLD!

AFTER THAT BIG PLAYTIME, MY MOM AND AUNTIE TAKE A NAP. AND NOW I PLAY WITH GRANDMA.

MOM WOKE UP WHILE
GRANDMA AND I WERE
PLAYING.

ARE YOU EATING A
SWEET FISH MOM?

IT'S GETTING LATE AND I
NEED TO GO TO SLEEP
AFTER SUCH
A BIG DAY!
I BRUSH MY TEETH TO
KEEP THEM HEALTHY.

GOODNIGHT MOM. THANK YOU FOR SUCH A WONDERFUL DAY.

I LOVE YOU SO MUCH!

AND NOW I'M READY TO SLEEP. WHAT A PERFECT ADVENTURE. I CAN'T IMAGINE A BETTER DAY THAN THE ONE THAT I HAD TODAY!

"GOODNIGHT PRINCE TORORO, SLEEP WELL." SAID, GRANDMA.

"TOMORROW I'M GOING TO TAKE YOU TO THE RIVER!"

THANK YOU, TO THE
LOUTRE OTTER CAFE
FOR LETTING ME
USE YOUR BEAUTIFUL
OTTERS FOR
THIS STORY.

THANK YOU
TORORO,
OTSUYU,
ODASHI,
WASABI,
NAMIDA.

FOR MAKING ME SMILE EVERY DAY.

THANK YOU TO ALL OF THE
OTTER FAMILY FANS!

PLEASE CONTINUE TO SUPPORT THEM!

HTTPS://WWW.LOUTRE-KYOTO.COM/

HTTPS://WWW.YOUTUBE.COM/C/LOUTRE